A NOTE TO PARENTS

When your children are ready to step into reading, giving them the right books—and lots of them—is as crucial as giving them the right food to eat. **Step into Reading**™ **Books** present exciting stories or information reinforced with lively, colorful illustrations that make learning to read fun, satisfying, and worthwhile. They are priced so that acquiring an entire library of them is affordable. And they are beginning readers with an important difference—they're written on three levels.

Step 1 Books, with their very large type and extremely simple vocabulary, have been created for the very youngest readers. **Step 2 Books** are both longer and slightly more difficult. **Step 3 Books,** written to mid-second-grade reading levels, are for the child who has acquired even greater reading skills.

Library of Congress Cataloging in Publication Data:
Hayes, Geoffrey. The mystery of the pirate ghost. (Step into reading. A Step 3 book) SUMMARY: Otto and his uncle Tooth track down the pirate ghost terrorizing Boogle Bay. 1. Children's stories, American. [1. Ghosts—Fiction. 2. Pirates—Fiction. 3. Mystery and detective stories] I. Title. II. Series: Step into reading. Step 3 book. PZ7.H31455My 1985 [E] 84-18228 ISBN: 0-394-87220-7 (trade); 0-394-97220-1 (lib. bdg.)

Manufactured in the United States of America 1 2 3 4 5 6 7 8 9 0

STEP INTO READING is a trademark of Random House, Inc.

Step into Reading™

THE MYSTERY OF THE PIRATE GHOST

by Geoffrey Hayes

A Step 3 Book

Random House New York

One morning in Boogle Bay
Otto and his uncle Tooth were cleaning
their attic.

"What's in that old trunk?"
Otto asked.

"Things I brought back from my
travels at sea many years ago,"
Uncle Tooth said.

4

Uncle Tooth opened the trunk.

He took out a shiny silver trumpet.

"I found this on Foghorn Island.
What an adventure that was!" he said.

"I wish I could have adventures,"
Otto said. "Nothing ever happens
around here."

Uncle Tooth gave Otto the trumpet.

"It's yours, if you want it," he said.

"Gee, thanks!" said Otto.

Otto blew on the trumpet.

Nothing happened.

He took a big breath and blew again.

This time the trumpet made
a little "fwee" sound.

"Keep trying," Uncle Tooth said,
"and you will get it right."

Otto ran outside with his trumpet.

Uncle Tooth's sister, Auntie Hick,
was hurrying down the path.
She did not see Otto.

"Fwee!" went the trumpet.

Auntie Hick screamed.

Uncle Tooth came running.

"I'm sorry, Auntie Hick," said Otto.
"I was just playing."

"Playing, my foot!" said Auntie Hick.
"I thought you were the ghost!"

"What ghost?" cried Otto.

"The ghost in my shop," she said.
"This morning I heard noises inside
my shop. I opened the door and saw—
a ghost! It stared at me with big red eyes!
I ran here as fast as I could."

"Don't be a fool," Uncle Tooth said.
"There are no such things as ghosts."

Auntie Hick stamped her foot. "I say
there are, because I've seen one."

Otto jumped up and down.

"Let's go find the ghost," he said.
"This might be the start of an
adventure."

The three of them hurried
up the path toward Auntie Hick's shop.

They passed Captain Poopdeck's
houseboat.

The captain was on the deck.
He was picking up wet laundry.

"Of all the rotten things,"
he muttered.

IRMA

8

"What's wrong?" asked Uncle Tooth.

"Someone stole my clothesline,"
said the captain.

"I'll bet anything it was the ghost!"
said Auntie Hick.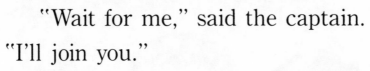

"What ghost?" cried the captain.

"There's a ghost on the loose
in Boogle Bay," said Otto.
"And we're going to catch it!"

"Wait for me," said the captain.
"I'll join you."

Soon they came to the inn.

Joe Puffin was standing on a stool
in front of the door. He had a cigar
in one hand and a scrub brush
in the other. He was screeching loudly.

"What's the matter, Joe?"
asked Uncle Tooth.

"Someone broke in here last night,"
said the puffin. "They turned everything
upside down. Then they did this."

He pointed to the door. On it was
a big red skull and crossbones.

"I'm sure it was the ghost,"
said Auntie Hick.

Otto told the puffin about the ghost.
"We're going to catch it. Want to help?"

"Count me in," said Joe Puffin.

They tiptoed to Auntie Hick's shop.
Uncle Tooth opened the door. They
peeked in.

Auntie Hick screamed.

There were boxes and jars, gumdrops
and jelly beans, all over the floor.
But there was no ghost.

"This ghost loves to make messes,"
said Uncle Tooth.

"Some detective you are!"
said Auntie Hick. "Any fool can see that!"

Then she began counting boxes.

"The ghost is a thief," she said.
"It took five boxes of saltwater taffy
and a deck of cards. This is serious.
What are you going to do about it,
Tooth?"

Uncle Tooth puffed on his pipe.

"I am going to the inn," he said.
"Food always helps me think."

Back at the inn Joe Puffin served up bowls of his special carrot soup.

"Delicious!" said Uncle Tooth. "Now, how will we catch this ghost? A thief returns to the scene of the crime."

"Do ghosts return too?" asked Otto.

"We will see," said Uncle Tooth. "We need something to lure it into our trap."

"I know," Otto said. "My trumpet!"

"Good thinking, Otto," said his uncle. "Now, here is what we will do..."

That night Otto put his trumpet
on the street outside the inn.
The trumpet shone in the moonlight.

Then Otto crawled inside a barrel.

Uncle Tooth hid in a doorway.

Captain Poopdeck crouched behind
the bar at the inn.

And Joe Puffin flew up to the roof
with a fishnet.

Midnight came and went.
Otto crept out of the barrel
and peeked around the corner.
He saw a giant shadow.
Was it the ghost?

No! It was Uncle Tooth.

"Shush!" Uncle Tooth whispered.
"The ghost is coming."

Otto held his breath.

The ghost bent down and picked up
the shiny silver trumpet.

18

"Now!" yelled Uncle Tooth.

Then he and Otto raced
around the corner.

Captain Poopdeck turned on
the lights in the inn.

The puffin flew from the roof
and dropped the fishnet
over the ghost.

The ghost slipped free of the net.
It ran down a dark alley.
Everyone chased it.
Then it disappeared!
Uncle Tooth scratched his head.
"Well, if that doesn't beat all!" he said.
"Maybe the thief really is a ghost."

"Look!" cried Otto.

He pointed to an open manhole
in the street.

Otto stuck his lantern down
the manhole. He saw something!
It was bobbing up and down in the
water.

Otto climbed down a ladder
and fished it out with his sword.

"A pirate's hat!" cried Uncle Tooth.
"This looks like old Blackeye Doodle's
hat to me."

"Didn't Blackeye drown at sea?"
asked Joe Puffin.

"That he did," said Uncle Tooth.
"But it would be just like him
to come back from the dead
to haunt us."

"And now he has my trumpet,"
said Otto sadly.

"We'll get it back," said Uncle Tooth.
"Tomorrow we will visit Widow Mole
at Deadman's Landing. She used to work
for Blackeye. Maybe she can give us
some clues. But now let's get some sleep.
I am as tired as an old boot."

The next morning Otto was up early.

He came downstairs with his sword, a map, a lantern, and a spyglass.

"You look all set for ghost hunting," said Uncle Tooth.

He opened the door.

"Look!" cried Otto.

There was a note pinned to the door with a knife!

Otto read it:

GIVE ME BACK MY HAT

OR YOU WILL BE SORRY!

It was signed "Blackeye Doodle."

Uncle Tooth snorted.

"I have seen many strange things in my day," he said. "But I never saw a note from a ghost before."

Uncle Tooth rowed his boat down
the coast.

Otto looked through his spyglass.
But the fog was so thick he could not
see anything. "This is spooky," he said.

"You are not scared, are you?"
asked Uncle Tooth.

"Of course not," said Otto.

WIDOW MOLE'S

POOL HALL

Soon they heard the tinkling sound
of a piano through the fog.
    They rounded a bend and docked
at Widow Mole's Pool Hall.

Uncle Tooth and Otto swung the door open and marched in.

The pool hall was filled with mean-looking sailors.

Some were playing pool.

Some were drinking beer.

Widow Mole was at the piano.

"Tooth! As I live and breathe!"
she cried. "What brings you here?"
"A ghost," said Uncle Tooth.
Widow Mole stopped playing
the piano.
The pool hall got very quiet.

Uncle Tooth showed Widow Mole
the pirate's hat.

"It's Blackeye's hat, all right,"
she said. "He was a mean pirate,
but a good friend. I'm sorry he is gone."

"We are not so sure he is gone,"
said Uncle Tooth. "He might even be here—
on Deadman's Landing. He used to hide
out here, didn't he?"

"Yes," said Widow Mole. "In a cave.
But I don't know where. It was his
secret."

"Thanks," said Uncle Tooth. "We
will have a look around."

30

Otto and Uncle Tooth walked outside—
and fell onto the dock!

Blackeye's hat flew out of Otto's hands.

The ghost grabbed the hat, put it on,
and faded into the fog.

"What happened?" asked Otto.

Uncle Tooth pointed to the door.

"See that rope across the doorway?" he said. "It is Captain Poopdeck's clothesline. We were tripped up by a ghost! You wait here for me, Otto. I am going to catch that ghost once and for all!"

He took the clothesline and headed for the beach.

Otto sat on the dock, but he soon got tired of waiting.

"I will walk down the beach just a little way," he thought.

After a while Otto found
a playing card stuck to a bush.
He moved the bush aside and saw
a little cave!

A bat flew out.

"Having an adventure is scarier
than I thought," he said.

Otto held out his sword, turned on
his lantern, and slowly walked
into the cave.

What a surprise!

In a corner of the cave were a bed and a trunk.

On the bed were playing cards and candy wrappers.

On the trunk was Otto's trumpet.

Suddenly Otto heard a bloodcurdling laugh.

He turned around.

The ghost was watching him
with its big red eyes!

Otto was trapped.

The eyes came nearer and nearer.

Otto grabbed the trumpet and blew on it as hard as he could.

"BLAAT!" went the trumpet.

The trumpet was so loud and so surprising that the ghost jumped and ran out of the cave.

It was so loud that Uncle Tooth heard it.

He came running down the beach.
"Otto! Are you all right?" he shouted.

"Y-y-yes," Otto said. "But the ghost
got away."

"There it is!" cried Uncle Tooth.

He pointed to the rocks above.
Otto looked up.

Something black peeked over the top
of the rocks.

"It's Blackeye's hat! After it!"
cried Uncle Tooth.

They climbed up the rocks.

But just as they got near the top,
the ghost stood up and jumped
off the cliff!

Uncle Tooth and Otto raced
to the edge and looked over.

In a cove below was a half-sunken
old ship. The ghost was running
across the deck.

Suddenly there was a loud CRACK!
The rotten wood broke apart.
The ghost fell through the deck
and—SPLASH!—right into the water.

Something else was splashing
in the water nearby.

"An octopus!" cried Otto.

"Help!" screamed the ghost.
"Don't let it get me!"

Uncle Tooth threw the clothesline
down. The ghost grabbed it. Otto and
Uncle Tooth began to pull him up.

The pirate's hat fell off and landed
on the octopus.

"Looks like Blackeye's hat has found
a new owner," said Uncle Tooth.

A very wet ghost stood before them.
"Now, take off that silly costume.
We know you are Blackeye Doodle,"
Uncle Tooth said.

"No, I'm not," said the ghost.
He took off his ghost costume.
"I'm his son, Ducky Doodle.
And I'm twice as tough as my pa."

"We'll see how tough you are in jail," Uncle Tooth said.

Ducky Doodle's face fell.

"Don't send me to jail," he begged. "Life in the orphanage was bad enough. I ran away to be a pirate like my pa."

Uncle Tooth shook his head.

"Listen, Doodle, a pirate's life is nothing but trouble. So far, you have upset people. You have stolen things. And you even lost your father's hat."

"I'm sorry," said Ducky Doodle. "But I don't know what else to do."

"Otto and I will show you how to earn an honest living," said Uncle Tooth.

"Okay," said Ducky Doodle. "I will give it a try."

Ducky Doodle did not go to jail.
But he did pay for his crimes.

First he returned the clothesline
to Captain Poopdeck—and washed
a tub of dirty laundry.

Next he told Joe Puffin that he was
sorry. Joe Puffin forgave Doodle,
but only after Doodle washed the dishes
and scrubbed the floor.

Then Otto, Uncle Tooth, and Ducky Doodle went to Auntie Hick's shop.

"This is the ghost," Uncle Tooth said. He told Auntie Hick the whole story.

"Well, I never!" Auntie Hick said.

"I will pay you back by working in your shop," said Ducky Doodle.

Auntie Hick thought about that.

"Well, I sure could use some help," she told Otto and Uncle Tooth.

"I'll see that he behaves himself," "And I'll teach him to read and write. I'm sure he didn't learn much in the orphanage."

Ducky Doodle groaned.

Auntie Hick let Otto and Uncle Tooth keep the rest of the stolen candy.

"It's not much of a reward," Otto said. "But we had fun."

"More fun than mending fishnets," said Uncle Tooth. "Maybe we could solve more mysteries."

"And have more adventures!" cried Otto.

So they did!

OTTO & TOOTH
FOR HIRE AS
DETECTIVE - ADVENTURERS
BY THE HOUR, DAY, OR WEEK